Ben's FAMILY

Written By Elliot Riley

Illustrated By Srimalie Bassani

Rourke
Educational Media
rourkeeducationalmedia.com

Before & After Reading Activities

Teaching Focus:

Concepts of Print: Have students find capital letters and punctuation in a sentence. Ask students to explain the purpose for using them in a sentence.

Before Reading:

Building Academic Vocabulary and Background Knowledge

Before reading a book, it is important to set the stage for your child or student by using pre-reading strategies. This will help them develop their vocabulary, increase their reading comprehension, and make connections across the curriculum.

1. Read the title and look at the cover. *Let's make predictions about what this book will be about.*
2. Take a picture walk by talking about the pictures/photographs in the book. Implant the vocabulary as you take the picture walk. Be sure to talk about the text features such as headings, the Table of Contents, glossary, bolded words, captions, charts/diagrams, or Index.
3. Have students read the first page of text with you then have students read the remaining text.
4. Strategy Talk – use to assist students while reading.
   - Get your mouth ready
   - Look at the picture
   - Think…does it make sense
   - Think…does it look right
   - Think…does it sound right
   - Chunk it – by looking for a part you know
5. Read it again.

Content Area Vocabulary
Use glossary words in a sentence.

cheer
helmet
stands
subway

After Reading:

Comprehension and Extension Activity

After reading the book, work on the following questions with your child or students in order to check their level of reading comprehension and content mastery.

1. *Why does Ben put on a helmet?   (Summarize)*
2. *Where do Ben and his mother live?   (Asking Questions)*
3. *How is Ben's family like yours? How is it different?   (Text to self connection)*
4. *What does Ben's family do at the park?   (Asking Questions)*

Extension Activity

Draw a picture of your family enjoying an activity together. Below the picture, complete this sentence:
My family likes to _____.

Table of Contents

Meet Ben

This is Ben.

This is Ben's mom.

They live in a big city.

There are many
things to see and do!

Ben and his mom take the **subway** to the park.

Game Time

Ben takes off his coat. He puts on his **helmet**.

Ben's grandparents arrive to watch.

"Have a great game, Ben!"
they say.

"Who is ready to play ball?" Ben's mom asks.

14

"We are, Coach!"
Ben's team says.

There are many families in the **stands**. They clap and **cheer** for the teams.

Pizza Party

After the game, Ben's team has a pizza party.

All of the families are there.

"Our team is like one HUGE family!" Ben says.

Ben loves his family.

Ben's family loves Ben.

Picture Glossary

 **cheer** (cheer): To praise or encourage with shouts.

 **helmet** (HEL-mit): A hard hat that covers and protects your head.

 **stands** (stands): An area for spectators to sit at a ballgame.

 **subway** (SUHB-way): An electric train that runs underground in a city.

Family Fun

Who are the people in your family?

Draw each person and write their name below their picture.

How is your family portrait like Ben's? How is it different?

About the Author

Elliot Riley is an author with a big family of her own in Tampa, Florida. She loves when everyone gets together to eat, laugh, and play games. Especially the eating part!

Meet The Author!
www.meetREMauthors.com

Library of Congress PCN Data

Ben's Family/ Elliot Riley
(All Kinds of Families)
ISBN 978-1-68342-316-4 (hard cover)
ISBN 978-1-68342-412-3 (soft cover)
ISBN 978-1-68342-482-6 (e-Book)
Library of Congress Control Number: 2017931165

Rourke Educational Media
Printed in the United States of America,
North Mankato, Minnesota

© 2018 Rourke Educational Media

www.rourkeeducationalmedia.com

Author Illustration: ©Robert Wicher
Edited by: Keli Sipperley
Cover design and interior design by: Kathy Walsh